This book belongs to

....

This edition first published in 2013 by Alligator Books Ltd.
Cupcake is an imprint of Alligator Books Ltd
Gadd House, Arcadia Avenue, London N3 2JU, UK
www.alligatorbooks.co.uk

Written by Katherine Sully
Illustrated by Frank Endersby

Printed in China 11455

Bobby Knows Best

cupcake

Bobby's friend Scoot came rushing to the burrow to find him.

"I saw a fox!" said Scoot. "A real live fox!"

Bobby had never seen a fox.

"Wow!" said Bobby. "What was it like?"

"It was...it was..." said Scoot, "...SCARY!"

Bobby thought Scoot was boasting.

When Scoot had gone home, Bobby went to find his mother.

"Mum," he asked, "have you ever seen a fox?"

"Oh dear me, yes," said his mother. "And I never want to see those big, sharp teeth again!" she added.

Bobby shivered.

"Stay away from foxes, Bobby," she sighed, "if you know what's good for you."

Bobby went to
find his Dad.

"Dad, have you ever
seen a fox?" he asked.

"Yes, son," said his father.
"A fox's big ears can hear you before you can see him!"

"Stay away from foxes, Bobby," he warned, "if you know what's good for you."

Bobby shivered.

Bobby asked his Grandma.

"Grandma, have you ever seen a fox?"

"A fox?" asked his grandmother, who was a little deaf. "I've seen a fox all right. And I've seen his big, sharp claws!"

Bobby shivered.

"Stay away from foxes, Bobby," she advised, "if you know what's good for you."

Bobby went to find his Grandpa.

"Have you ever seen a fox, Grandpa?" he asked.

"Oh, yes. If you see a fox, lad," said Grandpa, "this is what you do. Stay very still. Find the nearest bolt hole. Then thump your foot to warn the others and run for it. Don't run in a straight line, go in a zigzag – that'll slow old Mr Fox down all right!"

Bobby shivered.

That night, Bobby lay in bed. Everyone had a story about a fox except Bobby.

"I've got big ears too," he thought. "And big claws and teeth! I'm not scared of a fox!"

So Bobby crept out of the burrow into the moonlight and set off on a fox hunt.

The next morning, Bobby's mum called and called him for breakfast. She looked all around the burrow, but he wasn't there. Word soon went around the warren. No one had seen Bobby.

Finally, Scoot had a suggestion.

"I've got a funny feeling," said Scoot quietly," that he might have gone looking for a fox!"

A search party was organized.

Scoot was right. Bobby sat in a corner of the meadow, his ears wiggling and his nose twitching – because, in the other corner of the meadow there was a fox!

Now Bobby could see for himself.

The fox's ears were pointier than Bobby's.

The fox's teeth were sharper than Bobby's.

The fox's claws were longer than Bobby's.

Now Bobby was scared! Mum had warned him to stay away from foxes, and so had Dad and Grandma. Why, oh why, did he think he knew best?

Just then, out of the corner of his eye, Bobby saw a familiar pair of ears. Scoot's come to find me, thought Bobby, and now he's in danger too!

Bobby fixed his eyes on the fox and sat very still. The fox sniffed the air. More ears appeared above the grass. The rabbit search party spread themselves out across the meadow.

The fox was confused. But Bobby knew what he had to do. He remembered what his Grandpa had told him.

Bobby spotted the nearest bolt hole. He thumped his foot. At the signal, all the rabbits set off, running in every direction towards bolt holes hidden around the meadow.

Bobby ran for his life, zigzagging to give the others time to get away.

The fox chased this way and that, but he wasn't quick enough. Bobby dashed down the nearest bolt hole.

Back at the burrow, Bobby waited for his Mum and Dad to tell him off. But they were just happy that everyone was safe. And Grandpa even said, "Well done, lad! You slowed Mr Fox down all right!"

Later, Scoot came over.

"You were really brave!" said Scoot. "What a great fox story to tell the others!"

"Yes," agreed Bobby, "but I think I'll stay away from foxes from now on. It was...it was...SCARY!"

The End